SHERLOCK CHICK'S FIRST CASE

To librarians, parents, and teachers:

Sherlock Chick's First Case is a Parents Magazine READ ALOUD Original — one title in a series of colorfully illustrated and fun-to-read stories that young readers will be sure to come back to time and time again.

Now, in this special school and library edition of *Sherlock Chick's First Case,* adults have an even greater opportunity to increase children's responsiveness to reading and learning — and to have fun every step of the way.

When you finish this story, check the special section at the back of the book. There you will find games, projects, things to talk about, and other educational activities designed to make reading enjoyable by giving children and adults a chance to play together, work together, and talk over the story they have just read.

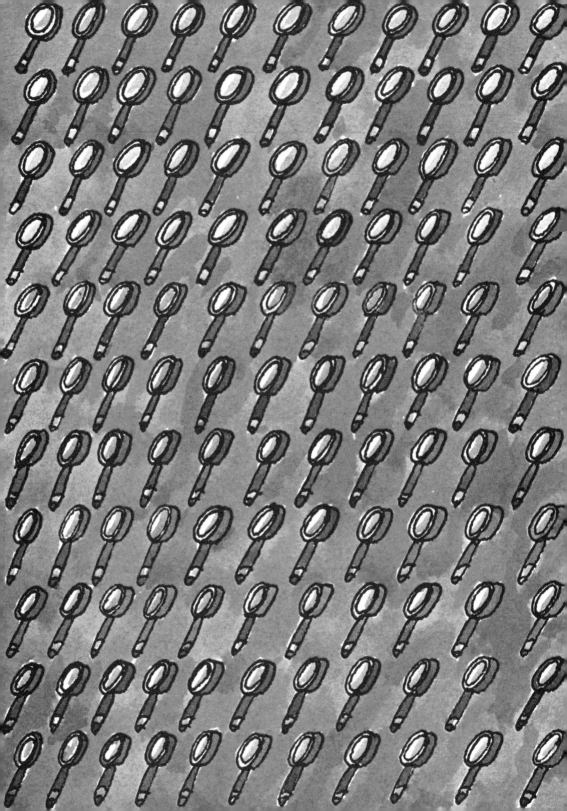

Parents Magazine READ ALOUD Originals:

Golly Gump Swallowed a Fly
The Housekeeper's Dog
Who Put the Pepper in the Pot?
Those Terrible Toy-Breakers
The Ghost in Dobbs Diner
The Biggest Shadow in the Zoo
The Old Man and the Afternoon Cat
Septimus Bean and His Amazing Machine
Sherlock Chick's First Case
A Garden for Miss Mouse
Witches Four
Bread and Honey

Pigs in the House
Milk and Cookies
But No Elephants
No Carrots for Harry!
Snow Lion
Henry's Awful Mistake
The Fox with Cold Feet
Get Well, Clown-Arounds!
Pets I Wouldn't Pick
Sherlock Chick and the Giant
    Egg Mystery

Library of Congress Cataloging-in-Publication Data

Quackenbush, Robert M.
    Sherlock Chick's first case / by Robert Quackenbush. — North American library ed.
        p. cm. — (Parents magazine read aloud original)
    Summary: Hatched from his egg with detective's hat and magnifying glass, Sherlock Chick immediately sets out to find who has stolen the corn from the chickens' feed bin.
    ISBN 0-8368-0892-4
    [1. Mystery and detective stories. 2. Chickens—Fiction.] I. Title. II. Series.
    PZ7.Q16Sk 1993
    [E]—dc20   92-32348

This North American library edition published in 1993 by Gareth Stevens Publishing, 1555 North RiverCenter Drive, Suite 201, Milwaukee, Wisconsin 53212, USA, under an arrangement with Parents Magazine Press, New York.

© 1986 by Robert Quackenbush. Portions of end matter adapted from material first published in the newsletter *From Parents to Parents* by the Parents Magazine Read Aloud Book Club, © 1988 by Gruner + Jahr, USA, Publishing; other portions © 1993 by Gareth Stevens, Inc.

Printed in the United States of America

1 2 3 4 5 6 7 8 9 98 97 96 95 94 93

SHERLOCK CHICK'S FIRST CASE

by Robert Quackenbush

GARETH STEVENS PUBLISHING • MILWAUKEE

PARENTS MAGAZINE PRESS • NEW YORK

The minute their chick was born,
Emma Hen and Harvey Rooster
knew that he was special.
He popped out of his shell
wearing a detective's hat.
"We'll call him Sherlock,"
said the proud parents.

Sherlock Chick's first words were,
"Are you in need of a detective?"
"Yes, we are," said Emma Hen.
"You've come just in time!"
She pointed to an empty
feed bin in the chicken yard.
"Someone has taken our corn!"

Sherlock Chick went
with his parents
to the feed bin.
"Who do you think took
the corn?" he asked.
"We don't know," said
his parents.

"I will look for clues,"
said Sherlock Chick.
He walked around the feed bin.
"Aha!" he said.

What did he see?

He saw a trail of corn.
It was leading out of the yard.
"I will follow this trail,"
said Sherlock Chick.
"I will find your corn
and bring it back."

"That's our boy!"
said his parents.

Sherlock Chick followed
the trail of corn.
Suddenly, he stopped.

What did he see?

He saw a horse.
"Do you like corn?"
asked Sherlock Chick politely.
"No," said the horse.
"Grass is my favorite
thing to eat."

The horse had not
taken the corn.
So Sherlock Chick
went on his way,
following the trail.
He stopped again.

What did he see?

He saw a goat.
"Do you like corn?"
asked Sherlock Chick politely.
"It's all right," said the goat.
"But eating the paper off cans
is much more fun."

The goat had not
taken the corn.
So Sherlock Chick
went on his way,
following the trail.
He stopped again.

What did he see?

He saw a pig.
"Do you always eat your
corn on the cob?"
asked Sherlock Chick politely.
"Yes," said the pig.
"The cobs are my favorite part."

The pig had not
taken the corn.
So Sherlock Chick
went on his way,
following the trail.
He stopped again.

What did he see?

He saw a scarecrow.
"Do you like corn?"
asked Sherlock Chick politely.
"I never touch it,"
answered the scarecrow.
"I'm here to chase crows away.
They like corn a lot."

"Aha!" said Sherlock Chick.
"I think I know who took
the corn from the
chicken yard."
He hurried on his way.
The trail of corn led to
an old barn and stopped there.
Sherlock Chick peeked
through a crack in
the barn door.

What did he see?

He saw three crows.
They were pecking away
at a pile of corn.
It was the corn from
the chicken yard!

Sherlock Chick had a plan.
He ran and got the horse,
the goat, the pig, and the
scarecrow to help.
They went with him
to the barn.

The horse put the scarecrow
next to the barn.
The goat knocked down
the barn door.
The pig ran through the barn
squealing, "Oink! Oink!"
as loud as he could.

The crows flew out of the barn and right into the scarecrow. "Awk! Awk! Awk!" they cried. They were so scared that they flew away and never came back.

Sherlock Chick and his friends
brought the corn back
to the chicken yard.
"This case is closed,"
said Sherlock.
Emma Hen and Harvey Rooster
were so happy to have
the corn back
that they had a big party
and invited everyone.

And that is the end of
Sherlock Chick's first case.

Notes to Grown-ups

Major Themes

Here is a quick guide to the significant themes and concepts at work in *Sherlock Chick's First Case:*

- Observation: it is important to look carefully and notice details about the world around us, as the reader is asked to do in this story.
- Being logical: Sherlock Chick works very hard to make sense of the clues he finds.

Step-by-step Ideas for Reading and Talking

Here are some ideas for further give-and-take between grown-ups and children. The following topics encourage creative discussion of *Sherlock Chick's First Case* and invite the kind of open-ended response that is consistent with many contemporary approaches to reading, including Whole Language:

- Six times in this intriguing story, the reader is asked "What did he see?" These are places to stop reading and examine the picture closely to try to find something that could be important to the little chick's mystery-solving efforts. Encourage your child to use his or her imagination to guess what is going to happen next.
- When investigating the animals' eating habits, Sherlock Chick asks all his questions *politely*. How do you say "Do you like corn?" politely? How do you say it rudely? Angrily? Jokingly? Why is it better to talk politely? Would Sherlock have gotten all the answers he needed if he had been rude?
- If the crows had merely asked (politely, of course) for some corn instead of stealing it, how might the story have ended?

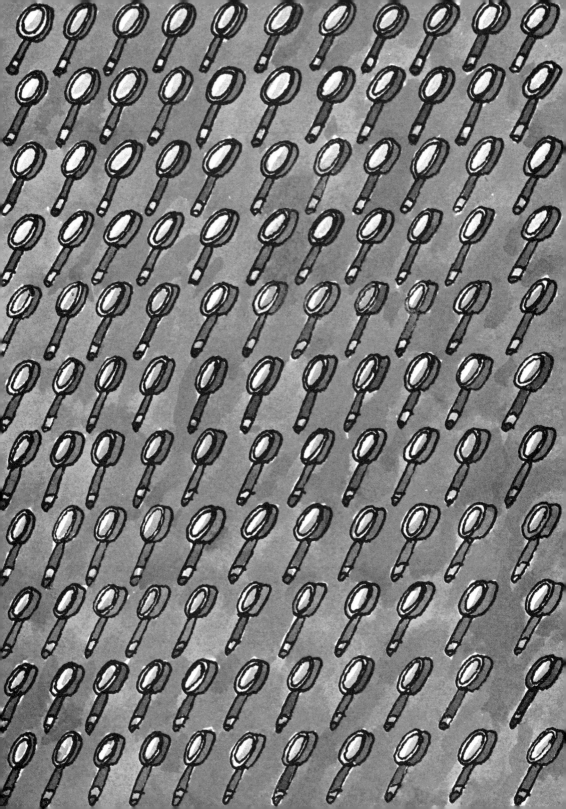

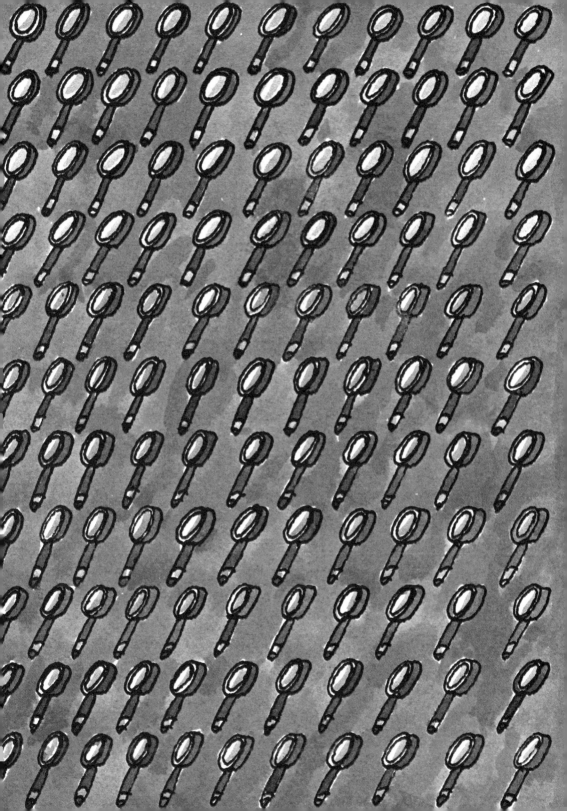

Games for Learning

Games and activities can stimulate young readers and listeners alike to find out more about words, numbers, and ideas. Here are more ideas for turning learning into fun:

Scavenger Hunt

Children love looking for clues and tracking down prizes, from looking for Easter eggs to going on scavenger hunts. Following a trail helps reinforce the kind of visual tracking and sequencing skills needed in more academic activities, such as reading and math.

A fun way to encourage your child to pay attention to visual detail and learn how to follow items in sequence is to make trails out of dried beans, peanuts in the shell, miniature chocolates or candy kisses, or any other small item easily "tracked" by your detective(s). Put a small treasure at the end of the trail. This can be as simple as a note of congratulations, a cookie, a toy, or a "ticket" to stay up late for a special television program. Provide a container, such as a paper cup or paper bag for your child to gather the "evidence" as she or he follows the trail. If you are making trails for more than one child, you can make each out of a different kind of edible item to avoid confusion and unnecessary competition. Make sure the items are equally appetizing: no dried beans if you are marking another trail with wrapped candy. In this game, everybody wins.

About the Author/Artist

When ROBERT QUACKENBUSH's son, Piet, was very small, he was curious about everything. In fact, he liked to walk around with a magnifying glass so he wouldn't miss anything! Remembering this helped Mr. Quackenbush create the Sherlock Chick character.

Robert Quackenbush has worked on more than 150 books for children. He has taught painting, writing, and illustrating to adults and art to children in New York.

DATE DUE			
OC 18			
T14			

E
Q

Quackenbush, Robert

Sherlock Chick's
first case

Anderson Elementary

 GUMDROP BOOKS - Bethany, Missouri